Volunteering

Amanda Rondeau

Consulting Editor
Monica Marx, M.A./Reading Specialist

Published by SandCastle™, an imprint of ABDO Publishing Company, 4940 Viking Drive, Edina, Minnesota 55435.

Printed in the United States.

Credits
Edited by: Pam Price
Curriculum Coordinator: Nancy Tuminelly
Cover and Interior Design and Production: Mighty Media
Photo Credits: Comstock, Digital Vision, Eyewire Images, PhotoDisc, Skjold Photography

Library of Congress Cataloging-in-Publication Data
Rondeau, Amanda, 1974-
    Volunteering / Amanda Rondeau.
      p. cm. -- (United we stand)
    Includes index.
    Summary: Explains different ways to volunteer to help people and how it can make a difference.
    ISBN 1-57765-882-5
    1. Voluntarism--Juvenile literature. [1. Voluntarism.] I. Title. II. Series.

HN49.V64 R655 2002
361.3'7--dc21
                                                                                    2002066402

SandCastle™ books are created by a professional team of educators, reading specialists, and content developers around five essential components that include phonemic awareness, phonics, vocabulary, text comprehension, and fluency. All books are written, reviewed, and leveled for guided reading, early intervention reading, and Accelerated Reader® programs and designed for use in shared, guided, and independent reading and writing activities to support a balanced approach to literacy instruction.

Let Us Know

After reading the book, SandCastle would like you to tell us your stories about reading. What is your favorite page? Was there something hard that you needed help with? Share the ups and downs of learning to read. We want to hear from you! To get posted on the ABDO Publishing Company Web site, send us email at:

sandcastle@abdopub.com

SandCastle Level: Transitional

What is volunteering?

Volunteering is helping others.

You can make a difference when you volunteer.

Cindy volunteers to bring
Ellen to the park.

Anyone can volunteer.

Brandy volunteers to recycle cans and papers.

Recycling helps the community.

Lucy volunteers to spend time with an older person.

It helps older people to have visitors.

Eva volunteers to spend time with animals at the animal shelter.

It helps the animals.

Rick volunteers to read to Steve.

It helps Steve learn to read.

Julie and Dawn volunteer to help build a house.

It helps a family that needs a home.

Mrs. Jones's class volunteers to plant trees in the park.

It helps the earth.

What is James doing to volunteer?

(recycling)

Index

Glossary

anyone   any person

community   any group of people living in the same area or having common interests

difference   the way in which people or things are not alike

family   a group of people related to one another

shelter   something that protects

volunteer   to offer to do a job, most often without pay

About SandCastle™

A professional team of educators, reading specialists, and content developers created the SandCastle™ series to support young readers as they develop reading skills and strategies and increase their general knowledge. The SandCastle™ series has four levels that correspond to early literacy development in young children. The levels are provided to help teachers and parents select the appropriate books for young readers.

Emerging Readers
(no flags)

Beginning Readers
(1 flag)

Transitional Readers
(2 flags)

Fluent Readers
(3 flags)

These levels are meant only as a guide. All levels are subject to change.

ABDO
Publishing Company

To see a complete list of SandCastle™ books and other nonfiction titles from ABDO Publishing Company, visit www.abdopub.com or contact us at:

4940 Viking Drive, Edina, Minnesota 55435 • 1-800-800-1312 • fax: 1-952-831-1632